MONSTER TROUBLE!

For Leo and Arielle Ghiloni—always remember to kiss your monsters. –L. F.

To my lovely mother, Carmelinda, who did a wonderful job raising six little monsters. –M. R.

ISBN 978-0-545-90653-1

12 11 10 9 8 7 6 5 4 3 2 1 15 16 17 18 19 20/0

Printed in the U.S.A. 40

First Scholastic printing, September 2015

Art direction and design by Merideth Harte

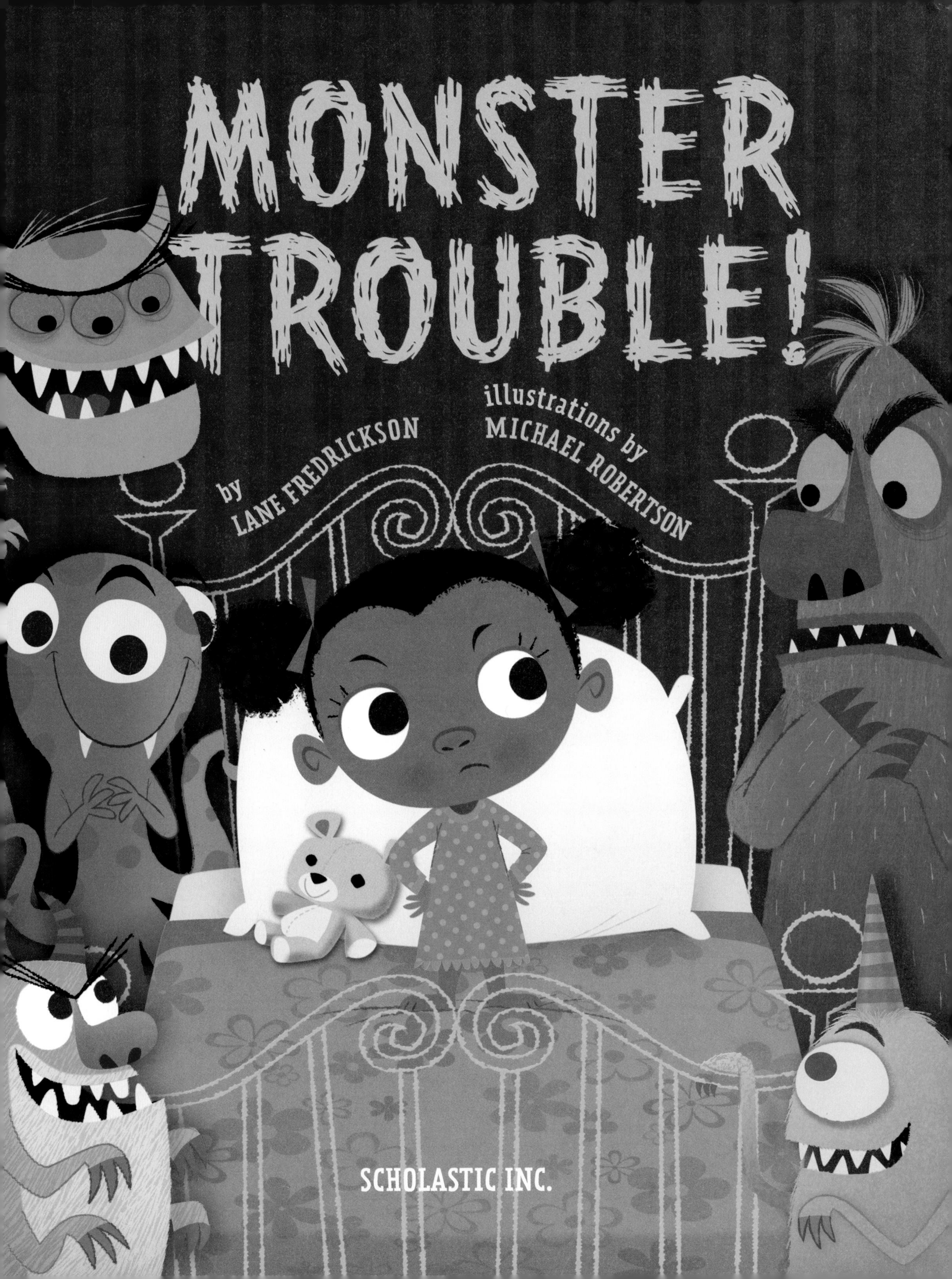
MONSTER TROUBLE!
by
LANE FREDRICKSON
illustrations by
MICHAEL ROBERTSON
SCHOLASTIC INC.

Winifred Schnitzel was never afraid.
Not of monsters or ghouls or the noises they made.

She loved scary movies and werewolves and thunder
and peg-legged pirates who bury their plunder.

Still, Winifred's bedtime was hardly spook-free.
The neighborhood monsters would *not* let her be.

Each night they'd show up and attempt to be scary.
Some would growl; some would belch. Some were slimy, some hairy.

Monster
Tails

But all of their monsterly mayhem was moot—
because Winifred Schnitzel thought monsters were cute.

Still, night after night, all those monsters kept creeping
into Winifred's room, interrupting her sleeping.

Too tired for math, too exhausted for fun,
she finally decided, "Those monsters are done!"

She ordered a book titled *Monsters Beware!*
and constructed the "Sticky-String, Small Monster Snare."

But *that* night, the BIG monsters all showed up first;
the Sticky-String Snare got so stretched that it burst.

There were monsters on bed posts and stuck to the wall.
They made slingshots from string: They were having a ball.

Winifred sighed. They were louder than ever.
She knew that she needed to try something clever.

So she brought in some stinky, old Limburger cheese.
The label said: CAUTION! MAKES BIG MONSTERS SNEEZE.

The monsters just called up the Goblin Street Deli.
They ordered in bagels and fish-eyeball jelly.

Winifred barely got through the next day.
She dozed off in art class and snoozed through ballet.

She decided, "That's it! I've got to get tough!"
She was tired of monsters. Enough was enough.

So she built every spook-trap in *Monsters Beware!*
and one of her own called "The Prickly Bum Chair."

Poor Winifred yawned. She was so very sleepy.
She was starting to look a bit spookishly creepy.

When the monsters showed up with their howling and roaring,
Winifred Schnitzel was already snoring!

SIT HERE
RELAX
TAKE A Load OFF

She was dreaming of puppies when a monster went HISS.
She reached out and gave it a big, sleepy KISS.

The monster yelled, "Yuck!" All the others were heaving.
One gagged. And a big monster shouted, "I'm leaving!"

Winifred knew that despite their uniqueness,
she'd discovered that monsters have one silly weakness.

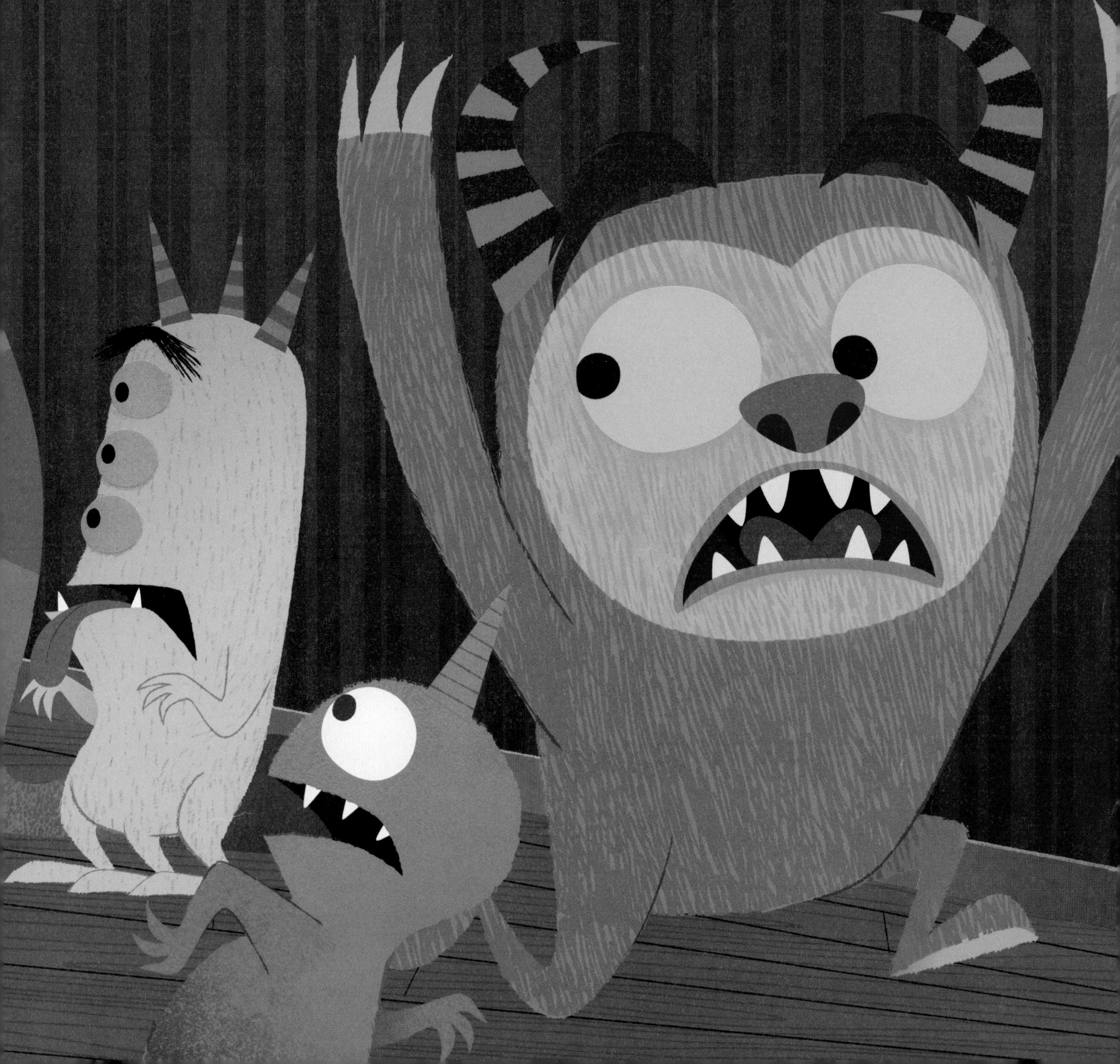

So she puckered and pouted and kissed them all good.
Those monsters screamed, running as fast as they could.

Now Winifred sleeps very soundly at night.
In the daytime, she's happy and perky and bright.

But sometimes she finds that a monster's crept in
right around bedtime, with a monsterly grin.

She ignores all the growling and roaring and hissing,
since the one thing that all monsters hate most is . . .